D1074619

For Trey... our hero

To all the parents, doctors, therapists (speech, occupational, physical), teachers, teacher aides, and members of the Department of Education who are doing their part to assist children who are autistic, developmentally delayed, suffer from ADHD, communication and/or speech delays, and more, we thank you for your service in improving the lives of the future of our country.

Special thanks to the staff of Tiegerman School (formerly The School for Language and Communication Development [SLCD]) in Glen Cove, New York. Your tireless dedication to our hero has made a world of difference.

Mrs. Debra Knight, for shining the light when others did not.

Mr. Gary Schatsky, for guiding us in the right direction.

Phylicia Johnson for helping to facilitate our journey.

Mascot Books for helping us bring our vision to reality.

Nidhom for turning our words into amazing illustrations.

www.mascotbooks.com

The Amazingly Awesome Amani

©2018 Jamiyl Samuels for W.R.E.a.C Havoc Enterprises. All Rights Reserved. No part of this publication may be reproduced, stored in a retrieval system or transmitted in any form by any means electronic, mechanical, or photocopying, recording or otherwise without the permission of the author.

For more information, please contact:
Mascot Books
620 Herndon Parkway, Suite 320
Herndon, VA 20170
info@mascotbooks.com

Library of Congress Control Number: 2017915897

CPSIA Code: PRT0618B
ISBN-13: 978-1-68401-610-5

Printed in the United States

W.R.E.A.C HAVOC HEROES PRESENTS

Written by **Jamiyl & Tracy-Ann Samuels**

Amani Taylor was a special boy.
He liked to go bowling and play golf and soccer, but his favorite thing to do was read books. He liked all kinds of books—books about animals, books about monsters—

but he especially loved books about superheroes. The Ninja Mutants were his favorite.

He also liked **Amazing Man**, who did cool things like fly high in the sky and save people who were in trouble.

Amani was ***very smart*** and did well in school, always getting **100%** on the weekly spelling quiz. But he kept to himself and didn't talk with the other kids. Even when some of the kids tried to speak to Amani, he didn't respond, he just smiled. The other kids thought he was a little different, and they often spoke about him behind his back.

The next day, Amani's teacher noticed he was sitting by himself, drawing with his crayons.

"What are you drawing, Amani?" the teacher asked.

Amani stopped drawing and showed his artwork to his teacher.

Every night at 8:00, Amani knew it was time to get ready for bed. He would take a bath, put on his pajamas, brush his teeth, and lay down in his bed to say his prayers. On this night, after Mommy kissed his sister Sandy goodnight, she noticed he was not happy.

"What's wrong, Amani?" Mommy asked. "Is something going on at school?"

Amani nodded.

Mommy leaned over and hugged Amani. "Listen, you are a very *special boy*," she said. "You are smart, you are loving, you are amazing! Don't let anyone tell you otherwise. Mommy and Daddy will always love you!"

Amani clasped his hands together. As his Mommy said the Lord's Prayer, Amani did not speak, but he was listening to every word.

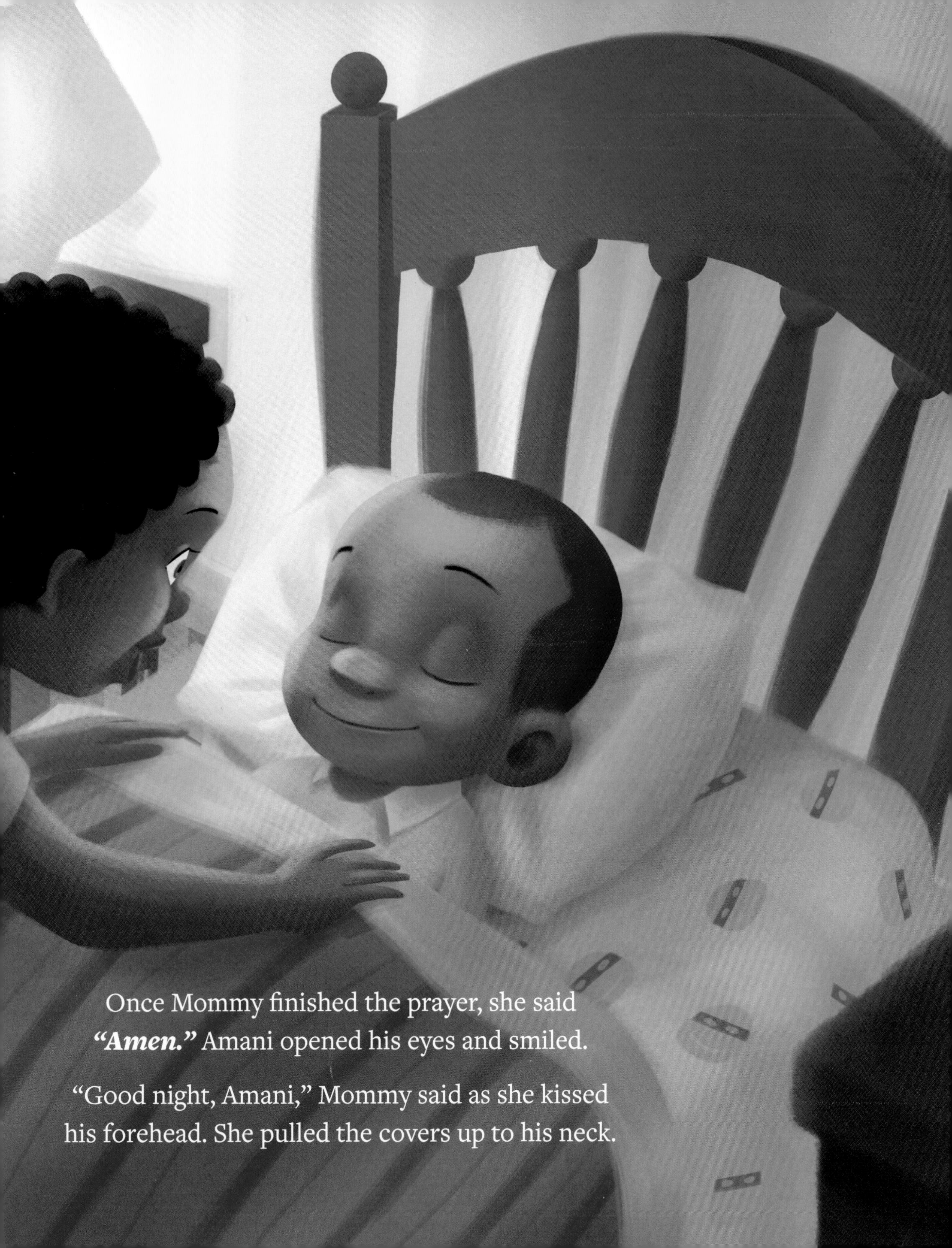

Once Mommy finished the prayer, she said ***"Amen."*** Amani opened his eyes and smiled.

"Good night, Amani," Mommy said as she kissed his forehead. She pulled the covers up to his neck.

“Heellp! Heeellllp!”

Amani opened his eyes and sat up. He looked over at his little sister Sandy, who was still wrapped in her Doctor Girl sheets. Amani jumped up from his bed and ran to the window. Two young boys were outside. One was taller and heavier than the other.

“HELP ME SOMEBODY!”

It was the smaller boy who was screaming. The taller boy was trying to take his ball. Amani knew he had to act fast. He ran into his closet. When he came out, he was dressed in a jumpsuit made of blue fabric with a green “A” painted on the chest. A red cape completed the outfit. The outfit of a superhero...

AWESOME AMANI!

AWESOME AMANI was ready to save the day, but first he had to figure out how to get outside. He couldn't walk out the front door, it was past his bedtime! He would have to go out the window. Too bad Amani couldn't fly like his favorite superhero, Amazing Man, but with his sister's jump rope he could climb down.

Amani carefully slid down the wall. As soon as he made it to the ground, Amani saw the taller boy wrestle the ball away from the smaller boy.

The taller boy ran away with the ball. Amani ran after him, but the boy was too far away.

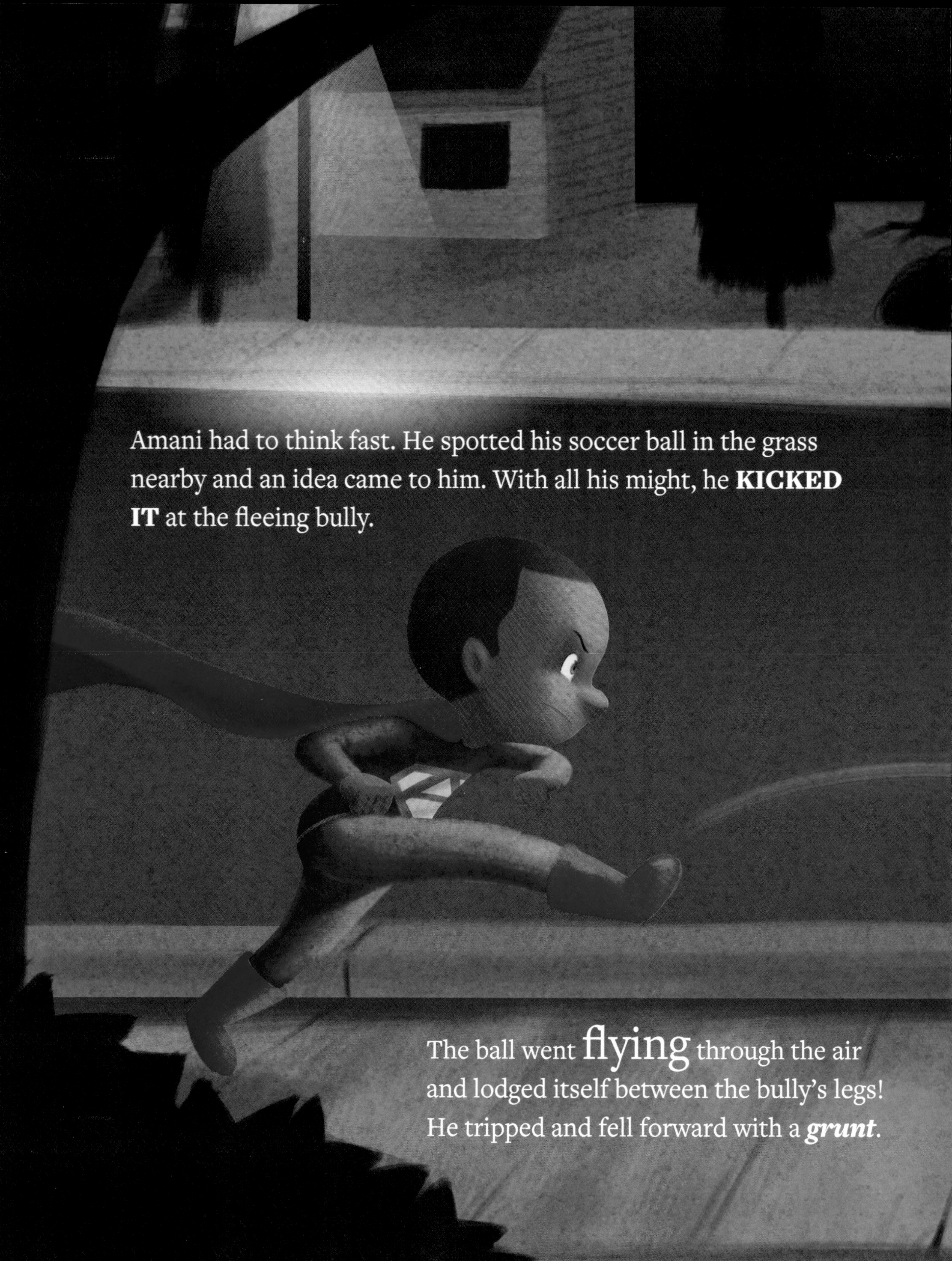

Amani had to think fast. He spotted his soccer ball in the grass nearby and an idea came to him. With all his might, he **KICKED IT** at the fleeing bully.

The ball went flying through the air and lodged itself between the bully's legs! He tripped and fell forward with a ***grunt***.

Amani ran up to the bully and took the ball back.

"Thank you so much," the small boy gushed as Amani gave back the ball. "THAT WAS AWESOME!"

"That's my name!
AWESOME AMANI!"

"Amani!"

That was his Mommy calling his name. Amani knew he had to get back to his room before Mommy and Daddy saw he was gone. Amani ran back down the street to the spot under his bedroom window, but when he got there, the rope was **gone!**

“Looking for this?”

He looked up and saw his little sister Sandy looking down at him with the rope in her hand.

“Sandy, give it back!” Amani pleaded.

He watched in horror as his little sister turned toward the bedroom door and yelled...

"MOM!"

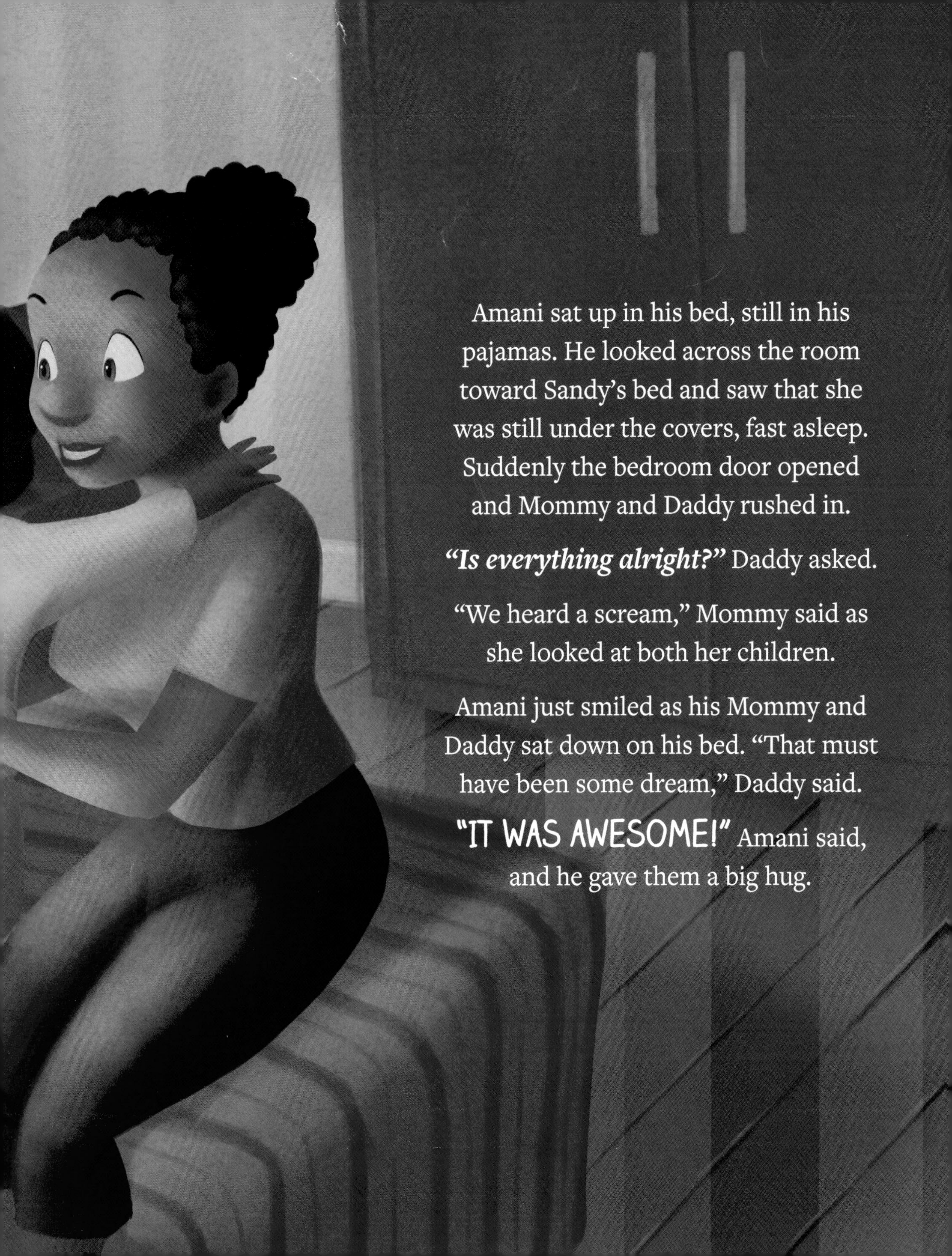

Amani sat up in his bed, still in his pajamas. He looked across the room toward Sandy's bed and saw that she was still under the covers, fast asleep. Suddenly the bedroom door opened and Mommy and Daddy rushed in.

"Is everything alright?" Daddy asked.

"We heard a scream," Mommy said as she looked at both her children.

Amani just smiled as his Mommy and Daddy sat down on his bed. "That must have been some dream," Daddy said.

"IT WAS AWESOME!" Amani said, and he gave them a big hug.

ABOUT THE AUTHORS

Jamiyl Samuels has been creatively writing for over 25 years. Whether it is screenwriting, making numerous contributions to entertainment magazines, blogs, and websites as a freelance writer, or creating poetry or song lyrics, Samuels continues to do what he loves while striving to make an impact with his work. He began his college career as a Theater major at **Morgan State University** in 1996, but ultimately graduated with a Bachelor's degree in English and a Master's degree in Media Arts with a concentration in screenwriting from **Long Island University** in Brooklyn, New York.

He is the founder of W.R.E.a.C Havoc Enterprises, a company that fosters growth, creativity, and education through informed written content, film, and recorded music. He is currently working on various projects and growing his small business online.

Tracy-Ann Samuels began her college career in 1996 studying Psychology at **Brooklyn College** before transferring to **Rutgers University Camden** campus in 1998 where she earned her Bachelor's degree in Psychology. She received her Master's degree in Social Work from **New York University**.

Her social work experience provides vital research and information as it pertains to materials dealing with children, families, and more. Tracy-Ann's ultimate goal is to assist at-risk children and their families, counsel couples through relationship and/or marital issues, and make an impact in her community.

The couple resides in New York with their two children.

Have a book idea?

Contact us at:

info@mascotbooks.com | www.mascotbooks.com

AWESO
MEAW
SOME
MEAW